Text and Illustrations

by Ellen C. Jareckie

Artist for House-Mouse Designs®

Dedicated to

All you "fellow mouse lovers"

out there!

Mudpie: Mudpie has brown fur and a nick in his left ear. His two favorite activities are eating and sleeping. He's a true mouse-potato. He could use a little exercise but isn't likely to begin a fitness routine anytime soon.

Amanda: Amanda has fawn colored fur and her ears are a bit large. She is the caretaker in the group. Amanda tends to be a bit bossy, though, truth be known, the others love that she takes charge.

Meet the Mice!

Monica: Monica is gray with a tiny body and big feet. She is very innocent and sweet. She is the baby of the group, which makes her a little bit spoiled. Spoiled with love and tenderness, but spoiled, nontheless.

Maxwell: Maxwell is reddish-brown in color and has a perpetually curled tail. He is rather mischievous and spends most of his time pulling pranks on the other mice.

WRITING
HISTORY
SEED SOWING
SPELLING
Reading
PUBLIC SQUEAKING
MATH
DRAWING

Muzzy: Muzzy is fuzzy. He has long hair that is mushroom gray/brown. He is the most curious of the five mice. Needless to say, Muzzy's favorite way to pass the time is investigating everything.

Mice have many faces
that change from time to time,
like Maxwell's bite of lemon
and Mudpie's bite of...

lime.

Everyone's attention is on the game above, while just below them all Monica is in...

Love.

surprised!

surprised!

sneaky.

When it's time for lunch
Mudpie isn't picky.
He'll eat all kinds of things
except a lunch this...

icky.

face!

sneeze!

The last piece disappeared and everyone's confused. Muzzy finds it shortly but he is...

not amused.

chilly.

shocked!

Mice think leaves are fun
for sailing off the ground.
Monica is joyful
until she dares look...

d
o
w
n.

grin!

confused.

yawn.

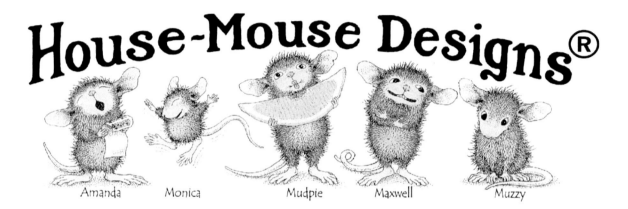

House-Mouse Designs®

Amanda Monica Mudpie Maxwell Muzzy

House-Mouse Designs, Inc
P.O. Box 48
Williston, VT 05495

www.house-mouse.com

Made in the USA
Middletown, DE
20 November 2018